P9-DJK-729

LITTLE POEMS
for
TINY EARS

POEMS BY
Lin Oliver

ILLUSTRATED BY
Tomie dePaola

Nancy Paulsen Books ◉ An Imprint of Penguin Group (USA)

NANCY PAULSEN BOOKS
Published by the Penguin Group
Penguin Random House LLC
Visit us at penguinrandomhouse.com

USA | Canada | UK | Ireland | Australia
New Zealand | India | South Africa | China
A Penguin Random House Company

Text copyright © 2014 by Lin Oliver. Illustrations copyright © 2014 by Tomie dePaola.
Penguin supports copyright. Copyright fuels creativity, encourages diverse voices, promotes free speech, and creates a vibrant culture.
Thank you for buying an authorized edition of this book and for complying with copyright laws by not
reproducing, scanning, or distributing any part of it in any form without permission.
You are supporting writers and allowing Penguin to continue to publish books for every reader.

Library of Congress Cataloging-in-Publication Data
Oliver, Lin.
[Poems. Selections]
Little Poems for Tiny Ears / Lin Oliver ; illustrated by Tomie dePaola.
pages cm
Audience: Age: 1–3.
Audience: Grade: Pre-school, excluding K.
Poems.
I. DePaola, Tomie, 1934– ill. II. Title.
PS3615.L84L58 2013   811´.6—dc23   2013014049
Manufactured in China.
ISBN 978-0-399-16605-1
Special Markets ISBN 978-0-399-17666-1 NOT FOR RESALE

7 9 10 8

Design by Marikka Tamura.
Text set in Archer Medium.
The art was done in transparent acrylics on handmade Arches 140 lb. cold press watercolor paper.

This Imagination Library edition is published by Penguin Young Readers, a division
of Penguin Random House, exclusively for Dolly Parton's Imagination Library,
a not-for-profit program designed to inspire a love of reading and learning, sponsored
in part by The Dollywood Foundation. Penguin's trade editions of this work are
available wherever books are sold.

For Anarres, the beautiful child
who inspired these poems.
—L.O.

For my "Pod'ner" Lin,
and Aiden, Anarres, Nicholas and Alexander,
Leon, Izzie, and all the other babies
whose faces and tiny ears have inspired me.
—T.deP.

I SEE A BABY

I see a baby in the mirror.

Lean in closer, see her clearer.

If I laugh or if I coo

Or blow spit bubbles, she does too.

She is such a copycat

And looks like me, imagine that!

TOES

Way down there at the end of my feet,

I've got ten toes; they're really sweet.

I can count them, make them wiggle.

When they're tickled, watch me giggle.

I dress them up in shoes and socks

And take them out for nice long walks.

I'll bet that you have ten toes too.

Can you count them like I do?

1 2 3 4 5 6 7 8 9 10

WALKING

Hey, look at me, I'm walking tall
On two legs, no need to crawl.
If I fall down, I don't mind
Because I land on my behind.

IN MY STROLLER

"Come on, toots," my parents say,
"A stroll will do us good."
And just like that, we're on our way
To cruise the neighborhood.

I see two cats and then a dog
Who barks as I ride by.
Oh, there's some girl out for a jog!
I wave and tell her hi.

It's cozy in my stroller seat,

Zipping down the block.

One day I'll use my own two feet,

And I won't roll, I'll walk!

MY NOSE

Upward from your feet and toes
You'll find a thing they call your nose.
It's in the middle of your face—
This is, I think, the perfect place.
For if it were inside your ear,
You'd find it very hard to hear,
And if it grew out from your knee,
How strange and silly would that be?

SNEEZE

A sneeze
Is a breeze
In
Your
Nose.

MY TONGUE

My tongue is pink
And wet, I think.
In and out it goes.

It's in my mouth
A little south
Of where you'll find my nose.

NOISY ME

Achoo, hiccup

Babble, burp

Gurgle, giggle

Snort and slurp.

Noises come and noises go.

They really put on quite a show!

Y FIRST WORD

My first word, what will it be?
Mama, Daddy, more or *me*?
I might say *baby, ball* or *puppy*—
Or hold my hands out and say *uppie*!

When I talk, I might say *bird*
Or maybe words you've never heard
Like *binko-gaga-whoopsie-goo*
Or *nummy-wawa-doo-be-doo*.

Now I only point and coo,
But I can't wait to talk to you!

DOGS

Why do dogs have hairy faces

And scratch themselves in funny places?

I wonder why they have wet noses.

To sniff me better, I supposes.

Some dogs are big and others small

And some don't look like dogs at all.

Never mind, they're my good friends.

They give me love that never ends.

MY CAR SEAT

First, my arms go in the strap,
Bag of cereal in my lap.
Buckle, click, I'm safely in—
Haul out, folks, let's take a spin.

MY HIGH CHAIR

I like to drop food from my chair.
It lands *kerplop*, but I don't care.
I watch it fall down to the floor.
It's so much fun, I toss some more.

My mom says no, my dad says please
Stop launching bits of toast and cheese.
They're right—I will try hard to stop.
But first . . . just one more small *kerplop*!

PEEKABOO

"Peekaboo,
I see you!"
That's what the grown-ups say.

To my surprise
They hide their eyes
Then, *poof*, they go away.

I do not know
Just where they go.
Their faces disappear!

Then in a while,
With great big smiles,
They're back and say, "I'm here!"

THE KITCHEN DRAWER

Watch me scoot across the floor.
I'm heading for the kitchen drawer
To knock the pots and pans around
And throw the dish towels on the ground.

I rattle pans and bang the pots
And make some noise . . . well . . . okay . . . *lots*.
The kitchen echoes with the sound,
Till Mommy laughs and says, "Pipe down!"

She puts the pots and lids away,
But I'll be back another day!

DIAPER TIME

Every time they change my diapers,

They have to clean me with those wipers.

They lift my legs up in the air

And show the world my bottom bare.

One day I will be diaper free.

Bring on those underpants for me!

BELLY BUTTON

Hey there, Mister Belly Button,
You just lie there doing nothing,
Taking up my tummy space.
Can't you find some other place?

MY MOBILE

La dee dum and la dee dee,

My mobile circles over me.

Dangling dinos, nubby sheep

Swirl round and round to help me sleep.

The happy music plays and then

I listen while it plays again.

More tinkling, twirling like a top.

Will my mobile ever stop?

A SNOOZE

When I snooze
I don't wear shoes
Or visit zoos
Or kangaroos.
I close my eyes
And see blue skies
And dream sweet dreams
Until I rise.

CATS

Cats are slinky, soft and furry,

And when they talk, they sound all purr-y.

It's fun when they come up to you

And cuddle up, like kitties do.

Y DADDY'S BEARD

My daddy's beard
Is really weird.
It scratches when you rub it.

But when he snuggles
Up to me,
Oh man, I really love it.

THE BATH

Rubber duckies, floating books,
Suds and bubbles, happy looks.
Bath time's full of games and fun,
Splishing, splashing till it's done.

Afterward, I'm squeaky clean,
The tidiest tot you've ever seen.
We dry me off and add some lotion.
I'm silky soft . . . a perfect notion!

BLANKIE

Without my blankie,
Me so cranky.
When it's by me,
Me all smiley.

Hush

In her favorite rocking chair
My mama holds me tight.
We rock and sway the hours away
Until we kiss good night.

Lin Oliver is the *New York Times* bestselling author of over twenty-five books for children. Known for her comic invention and light touch, she has created such series as Hank Zipzer, Ghost Buddy, Almost Identical and Sound Bender. An accomplished writer and producer of family entertainment, Lin is also the co-founder and executive director of the Society of Children's Book Writers and Illustrators. She lives and works in Los Angeles, where she eats tacos and walks on the beach.

www.linoliver.com

Tomie dePaola is the acclaimed author and/or illustrator of more than 200 books for children. He has received the Laura Ingalls Wilder Award, a Newbery Honor for *26 Fairmount Avenue*, and a Caldecott Honor for *Strega Nona*. He was awarded the Smithson Medal and the Regina Medal, was designated a "living treasure" by the state of New Hampshire, and received the 2012 Original Art Lifetime Achievement Award from the Society of Illustrators. He lives in New London, New Hampshire.

www.tomie.com